A Gift For:

the Yellow Door

From:

Sophie GAO

To all those who choose love instead of fear
—J.B.

To my husband Reino, and to Julia, Frans, and Veeti,
who keep me inspired
—A.L.H.

Please visit the author's web site
www.johnbucchino.com

Grateful
"Grateful" words and music by John Bucchino
Copyright © 1996 by John Bucchino
Art Food Music owner of publication and allied rights throughout the world
(administered by Williamson Music).
International Copyright Secured.
All Rights Reserved.
Illustrations copyright © 2003 by Anna-Liisa Hakkarainen
Manufactured in China by South China Printing Company Ltd. All rights reserved.
www.harperchildrens.com

Library of Congress Cataloging-in-Publication Data
Bucchino, John.
    Grateful: A song of giving thanks / by John Bucchino ; illustrated by Anna-Liisa
Hakkarainen.
        p.   cm.
    "The Julie Andrews Collection."
    Summary: An illustrated version of John Bucchino's song—giving thanks
and celebrating the gifts of life.
    ISBN 0-06-051633-X — ISBN 0-06-051634-8 (lib. bdg.)
    1. Children's songs—United States—Texts.   [1. Gratitude—Songs and music.
2. Songs.]   I. Hakkarainen, Anna-Liisa, ill.   II. Title.
PZ8.3.B8453 Gr   2003
782.42164'0268—dc21   2002003148
                                                                        CIP
                                                                        AC

Typography by Jeanne L. Hogle
1 2 3 4 5 6 7 8 9 10
❖
First Edition

Grateful

A Song of Giving Thanks

By John Bucchino • Illustrated by Anna-Liisa Hakkarainen

HarperCollinsPublishers

I've got a roof over my head.

I've got a warm place to sleep.

Some nights I lie awake counting gifts

Instead of counting sheep.

I've got a heart that can hold love.

I've got a mind that can think.

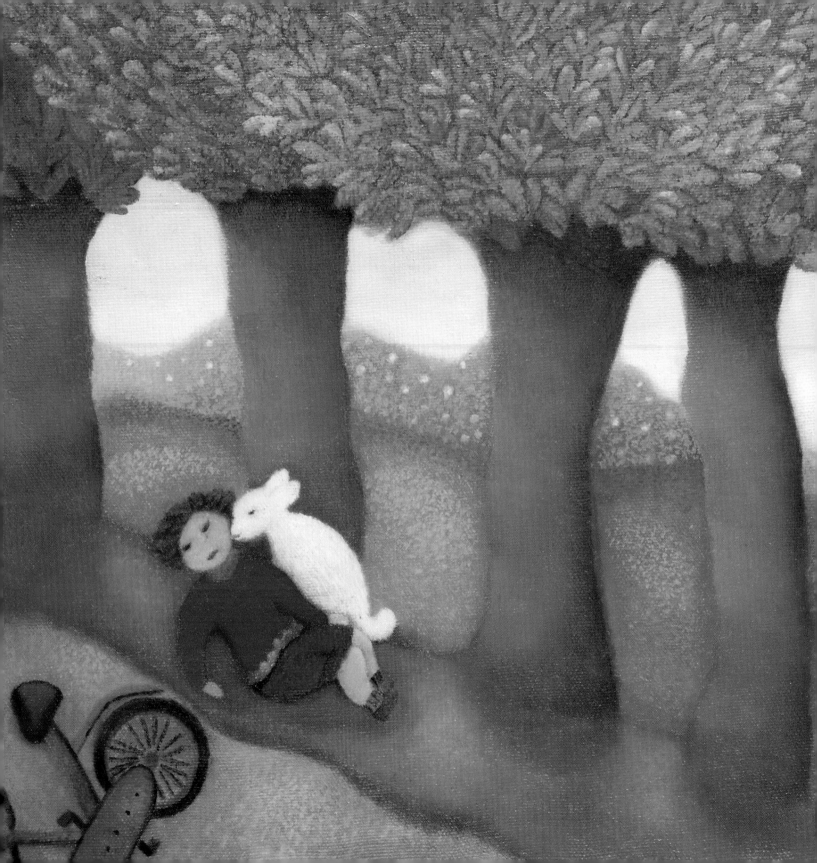

There may be times when I lose the light

And let my spirits sink . . .

But I can't stay depressed

When I remember how I'm blessed!

Grateful, grateful

Truly grateful I am.

Grateful, grateful

Truly blessed

And duly grateful.

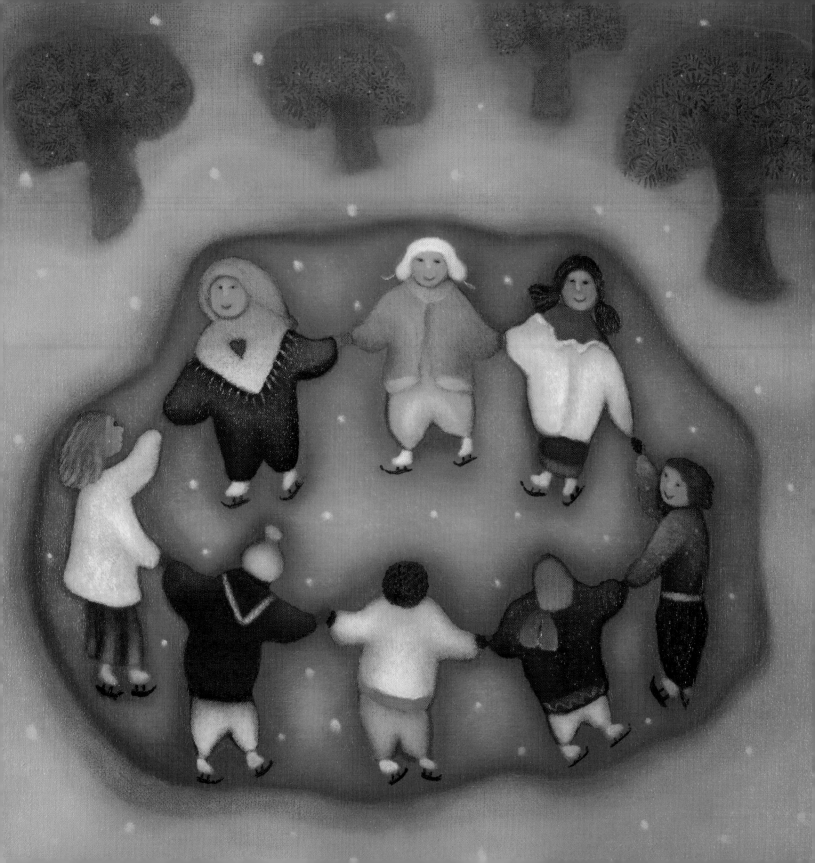

In a city of strangers,

I've got a family of friends.

(No matter what rocks and brambles

fill the way,

I know that they will stay until the end.

I feel a hand holding my hand.

It's not a hand you can see.

But on the road to the promised land

This hand will shepherd me . . .

Through delight and despair,

Holding tight and always there.

Grateful, grateful

Truly grateful I am.

Grateful, grateful

Truly blessed

And duly grateful.

It's not that I don't want a lot,

Or hope for more or dream of more.

But giving thanks for what I've got

Makes me so much happier than keeping score.

In a world that can bring pain,

I will still take each chance . . .

For I believe that whatever the terrain

Our feet can learn to dance.

Whatever stone life may sling,

We can moan . . .

Or we can sing!

Grateful, grateful

Truly grateful I am.

Grateful, grateful

Truly blessed

And duly grateful.

Truly blessed

And duly grateful.

Grateful

Words and Music by
JOHN BUCCHINO

NOTE: This is a simplified version of the sheet music of the song "Grateful." The complete version may be found in the songbook
GRATEFUL: The Songs of John Bucchino, available at www.johnbucchino.com